The Evening Before Christmas

Merry Christmas, Love, Always A heartwarming holiday love story.

Written By Dr. Alex

Table of Contents

Summary

Winter was not the time for everyone. Especially not for Holly, who was snowed in her college building. To her bad luck, she had decided to leave for home on the twenty-first, unlike her friends, when a snowstorm had suddenly hit town. She had cursed mother nature's name.

All she had wanted to do was get home as late as possible to shorten the time she would have to spend with her mum and stepdad... but now, she would never get to her destination in time. According to the news, the snowstorm would last days, the consequences might even weeks.

And being the only one in her college building could become very lonely... but maybe she wouldn't be as alone as she had expected. To make everything better, Cade Thindal hadn't gotten his ride back home either.

One

I opened the white curtain in my college dorm room. It was late, and the night was black.

Heavy accumulations of snow fell on the ground, turning the grey concrete white. Putting my lips together, I pushed my phone to my ear. The other person's voice came off as anxious, with an edge of blame bringing their tone up harsher.

"Holly, what are you going to do? Holy crap, are you starving to death?

I leaned against the wall with my back on the window seat. As I sat with my back to the window, I could see that the snowflakes were still falling steadily. I should have known the whiteout wouldn't end that soon. It was reported as such.

I bit my lip and responded, "I don't know, mama." It took all I had to resist the urge to chew my nails. When I was scared, I would fall into that awful habit, and I knew I'd never be able to stop.

I was confused by your "you don't know" response. Whether you need assistance, have you seen if somebody in the area is available to provide it? My mind's eye could practically make out the sound of her feet pounding the floor of our studio flat. When I eventually got home, I'm sure I would be able to make out her footprints. Of course, that's assuming I ever do. There was no sign that the snowfall would end any time soon.

It's peaceful in the hallways. I believe I'm the last one here.

Nothing was heard from the other end. As I spoke, I reached over to my left side and picked up the phone, moving it to my left ear. I sighed and rested my head against the chilly glass. I felt her blazing rage even though it was chilly outside.

“Mom?”

The other end of the telephone was either silent or filled with angry shouts. The moment Arthur's voice rose, I waited with my eyes rolling. They started fighting again. That's it, just what I needed at this moment. I waited until the twenty-first to go so I could escape their bickering.

And now I could hear it while driving in the car. How awesome.

I warned you she'd figure out a way not to show up. How come you wouldn't simply let me grab her?

Oh, you're putting me in the middle of this, huh? How the hell was I expected to know that a freaking storm was on the way?

Again, I shook my head and moaned.

Time would pass while this transpired. Times ranged from minutes to hours.

I removed the handset from my ear and ended the call. After putting it into flight mode, I set it down next to me. I knew there wouldn't be any good reception, but I preferred to avoid any unpleasant surprises. Eventually, my mom tracked out a fax machine and was able to get in touch with me again.

But they might easily forget about me for the time being.

I never saw the point in their marriage.

Perhaps they loved one other back when I was too little to remember, but that still didn't explain why they stayed together today. Years of incessant bickering and yelling flooded my memory. When I last saw them together, they hadn't even kissed or held hands.

As far back as high school was concerned, they never even attempted to behave like any of the other parents. There were other damaged families, but at least those people pretended everything was alright. They did it for the sake of their children, but I saw every awkward contact.

Intestines rumbled. I did not want to see anything, so I shut my eyes. I figured I should check to see whether there was still food after all this time had passed. If there wasn't, I'd be doomed. The chocolate bars and water bottles I had taken from the cafeteria earlier were still in my possession, but they wouldn't last forever. I needed more than this if I was ever going to make it out of this situation.

Ok, so maybe I'm being a little theatrical, but who among us wouldn't lose our minds in such a situation?

To the contrary, I planted my feet firmly on the floor and tucked my phone down the side of my flannel trousers. After putting on my slippers, I walked to my bedroom. The thought of taking the lengthy, dark route to the cafeteria made me moan.

I used some bobby pins to hold my hair in a low bun. Next, I slipped a jacket over my extra-wide black t-shirt. Even though I had turned up the heat to its highest setting in my room, it didn't imply the hallways would be any cozier. It was usually quite cold in the winter.

I got up and went to my dresser, where I looked for a flashlight. I didn't feel like going to the cafeteria just so I could use the restroom and drain my phone's battery. It was worn out, and I used it up faster than I could.

I locked the door behind me, grabbed my keys, and slung my bag over my shoulder. The lights outside in the snow were the sole source of illumination, and they were the only ones that could be seen from the passageway. Since I was alone myself, the building did seem like something out of a horror movie.

As I bolted the door behind me, my hands shook violently. I just couldn't take the chance of someone breaking in. Regardless of how long I had to wait before I was able to eat.

When I was ready, I swallowed and turned on my flashlight. I checked to the right and left to be sure nobody has hidden anywhere. I was being quite pitiful. Extremely and unreasonably pathetic. But there was nothing I could do about it.

Let it be known that I was terrified and that I had no qualms about saying so.

With one more inhale, I veered to the left and set off along the halls.

It was only the wind and my footsteps and I was completely alone. also, my living, pulsating heart. I had to take a deep breath. The only other person in the room was me. Who in their right mind would remain till now?

Truth be told, I was, but it wasn't the worst move I'd ever made.

If I had enough to eat, I may even learn to appreciate my alone here... I had never before minded being alone, so what was the big deal?

Perhaps it was because it was late at night. It was terrifying in the dark, but all I could do was shine a lamp on the route. I was too timid to go around the school looking for the light switches since I didn't know where they were.

Just some meal and then I was going to be in my room for the next several days. Within the confines of my home, I needed nothing else. At least, that's what I kept telling myself.

There was no way I could have lied to myself. Indeed, I was a miserable being.

Even the tiniest shock is enough to knock me down in a flash. When the wind picked in speed, it sent shivers down my spine. I figured it must be the case.

All I could see was snow falling, but it seemed like someone was repeatedly beating on the large windows.

My fist tightened around the torch in my hand.

Having this would allow me to f*ck whoever it is. Perhaps a good whack upside to the noggin would do the work. In the end, blood wasn't strictly necessary... The thought made me want to throw up. There was no use in my attempting to deceive myself.

If someone I didn't know was in here with me, I'd probably start weeping. As fast as my little legs could take me, I'd scream and run as far away as possible.

After that, I swung to the left and went around the bend.

To put it bluntly, I wasn't the quickest runner in the world because of my short legs. In no area was I a standout. Of course, I had successfully navigated my way into higher education without ever receiving a failing grade, but that was only because I put in a lot of effort.

It seemed that no matter how hard I tried, I could never accomplish everything that I had set out to do. The only trophy I could remember winning was a

spelling bee in second grade, and even that was a distant memory.
If I could just get here on my own, that would do. Late at night, though, I would still feel like a total failure.

When I turned the second bend to the right, I could see my ultimate destination. The cafeteria's doors, built of heavy, black wood, were massive. In my mind's eye, they'd always been towering above me.

After a brief pause, I laughed and reached for the door's golden knob. As a result, I yanked.

However, it seemed like nothing was happening.

What the f***, I said under my breath.

I yanked and yanked, but it was of no use. The pounding of my heart against my ribs became more painful.

My volume level increased. A loud "Fuck, fuck, fuck!"

To be honest, I didn't care if I screamed at this point. Even though no one was there, I was unable to unlock this door.

And here I was, thinking I was the only one: "And I thought I was the only one," I heard a voice behind me giggle. My stomach dropped to my feet and all I could do was scream bloody murder before I twisted around.

Two

It was pitch black and all I could hear was the rapid rhythm of my heart and the gasps of air as it from my lungs. As I fell backward, my back slammed against the solid wood door. Although the door handle dug uncomfortably into my back, I paid it no mind.

The wind carried the sound of someone laughing.

When I saw what was happening, I shivered and fumbled with my flashlight. Too busy to do anything else, I looked forward nevertheless. This is just my luck?

My mother's argument with my uncle Arthur would be the last thing I'd ever hear if I were to die. That was something that I just couldn't allow to take place. It didn't matter; I was going to die a loner.

Do you feel frightened after hearing my question? An oddly familiar voice laughed.

Tightening my hold on the torch, I raised it till I could see the layout of the people in front of me. One who is both tall and slim. The man seemed familiar, but I didn't know whether I could trust my intuition just now. So that I could better examine his eyes, I raised the torch.

A swift movement caused him to swivel to the side, his palm covering his eyes. No need to blind me, he screamed. He shambled over to the side, away from the spotlight I'd been beaming on him.

However, I was right behind them with the torch.

I had to learn his identity.

"Holly!"

A breath of fear escaped my lips.

It was a voice I had heard before. I knew it for a fact, but I couldn't put a name to the certainty.

When did I last see him?

Hopefully, he wasn't another college jerk as so many others have been... I wouldn't be able to cope with it for the following several days. It's horrible that the two of us would be trapped here.

As in, "Holy crap! It's me, Cade!"

Everything inside of me seemed to stop moving. Cade?

After a few seconds of this, I shook my head and let out a deep breath, my pulse racing. In the unlikely event that it was feasible. “Who?”
The man shook his head, raised his hands, and swiveled around to face me. I angled the torch beam so it hit him square in the face, but he didn't flinch this time. Squinting his eyes against the brightness was all he could do. Cade Thindal here. The person who was good at arithmetic in school. I'm going to be in the rear, and you can have the front.

I wrinkled my brow in concentration. Maths? I don't know why, but I just couldn't recall his face at the time.

I gulped some air down.

Taking in more of his features, I could make out a familiarity there. Or more about that, his hair. For some reason, I'd never taken the time to study his face. I could make out the little curve of his nose, and his eyes seemed to be the same dark color as his hair.

Many of the little brown patches on his face were concentrated on his nose.

Nonetheless, I had to check my assumptions to make sure I wasn't wrong. Is there a teacher here?"

His forehead wrinkled. “What?”

I gritted my teeth. "Who is our instructor if you are in my class?"

His brows furrowed, and a smile formed on his face. “You don’t know who I am, huh?” he laughed. OK, it's Mrs. Quinn. Even I couldn't get the old hag to remember my name. That's something you have in common.

Relaxing, I took a few deep breaths. My lips started to twitch into a grin. The old hag... What an asshole.

There was a brief moment of silence between us. A question: "Why are you even here?" My question came when I lowered the beam of light a little.

Not that I intended to, but he was completely blind.

A step forward, arms crossed, he made his position clear. I looked around to find the source of the commotion. No way would you be able to act like that and not be recognized, Holly.

While snorting, I noticed my face starting to become hot. Perhaps I had been yelling...

It was fortunate that the lighting conditions prevented him from seeing my face. By this point, I was certain that my face was completely flushed. As you can see,

my fair complexion made it impossible to conceal any makeup. It was quite annoying to me. Unfortunately, I didn't get my dad's tan or his somewhat darker skin tone.
Only pictures of us taken when I was two years old survived. On my dresser is one in which he is seen flinging me into the air. Mom was standing off to the side, smiling as she watched. We gave off the impression of being a contented bunch.

Then suddenly, it all started to come apart.

I said, "I thought I was alone," as my left hand began to twitch on the sleeve of my jacket. I shrugged my shoulders and made an effort to divert my attention. Just focusing on the present was my go-to.

Smiling and shaking his head, Cade chuckled. You and I both did, Holly. till I heard your sweet voice yelling "fuck" over and over again. In an offhand way, he cocked his head. For what purpose were you using that time?"

To show my disapproval, I tightened my lips. "I was attempting to get nourishment."

He arched a brow in thought. The corner of his mouth turned up in a smile. "Were you locked out?"

I closed my eyes and took a long breath. I gave a simple nod in agreement.

“So, that’s what the shouting was all about.”

This caused me to sigh. In addition, I nodded once more at that point.

From now on, I'll refer to him as mister oblivious. Would you like some assistance?

For an instant, I turned around to check the exit. I wrinkled my brow in concentration. Basically, "It's locked."

"I'm aware of it as well, Holly." He got up and began to stroll my way. I shifted to the side as he walked. I needed some distance from you. Just thought we attended the same class didn’t indicate that we knew each other.

He may be a killer for all I know.

The doors to the restrooms are always locked.

I squeezed my jaws together and stared as someone kneeled in front of the door. What gives you that idea?

He just shrugged and sent me a glance. Inquiring minds want to know, "What is logic?"

My arms were crossed as I snorted. How rude.

"Could you shine a light on this for me?"

When the signal was given, I kidded stood, and raised the flame.

After a few seconds of what seemed like nothing, I heard a click and realized he was doing something. He swiveled around on his buttocks to face me. He flashed me a devilish grin. Nothing is secure anymore; all the doors are open.

As he got to his feet, he put a hand down to steady himself. His mouth twisted into a gasp as he stretched. There were loud cracks, and I cringed.

What I mean is, "Doesn't it hurt?"

He brushed off my inquiry and yanked on the door instead. The door creaked open as it opened. And you didn't believe I could do it, he teased, shaking his head. I wanted nothing more than to wipe that grin from his face.

It damaged my confidence to see him so confident in himself.

The fact that he was able to access it, however, raised more inquiries.

My eyes squinted and I swiveled my head to direct the light back toward his face. He squinted his eyes and his face to avoid the light. Laughing was difficult to suppress.

A glance at him told me he was too foolish to be real.

You think it humorous, right? As a result, he granted. When he saw me he shook his head.

“Very.”

Even so, he was trying to force a grin. It was clear to me.

I gave a little shake of the head and stepped forward. A question: "Why are you even here?"

Again, he wrinkled his brows. "You asked that already."

I groaned and said, "And now, I'm asking again, since you didn't give me the response I wanted. It seems like you should be home by now.

I could ask you the same thing.

My eyeballs rolled. “Cade.”

He gave a casual shoulder shrug. He said, "The storm came and I missed my bus." "I'm guessing it's the same for you, too?"
With a mumbled, "Yup," I agreed. I had my doubts as to whether or not he was speaking the truth, but I didn't give a hoot. This was the cue for my stomach to resume its growling.

When Cade started laughing, I think my cars flushed pink.

Without a word, he walked inside the cafeteria and vanished. I waited patiently. I wasn't sure whether I should follow him or not. I recoiled when the wind slammed against the glass panes. I couldn't even laugh at how jumpy I was.

I put my left arm about my middle and shook my head. I needed to move through this as soon as possible. The good news was that I was no longer completely alone. And I had no reason to think Cade would harm me. Perhaps I was only hoping against hope. Just about everything is possible... Well, if-

Will you continue to wait or will you be arriving soon? Cade yelled out of the café.

I straightened up and started jogging after him, my flashlight illuminating the path.

Three

"What's with all the locks?" Shaking my head, I muttered under my breath as I scanned the cafeteria. I had my hands resting on my hips. I was fuming with annoyance.

The kitchen door was locked as well.

It was a spacious area, with tall walls and enormous windows, that served as the cafeteria. This location has long been one of my favorites. The one at my university was considerably roomier and cozier than the one at my high school.

If there was time, my coworkers and I would dine here at lunch. The years had made one of the tables ours. That one was stationed close to the entrance we'd just used.

Softly grinning, I glanced over at it.

The situation would be much better if they were present.

I wish I could have been here with them since I think we would have had a blast being alone. We would have gone looking for hidden treasure, shared ghost tales, and maybe imbibed till the wee hours of the morning... Like we didn't do it all the time.

But we could have had much more fun if nobody had been able to stop us. Some of our instructors, like Mrs. Quinn, would be furious to discover us under the influence of alcohol.

My own experience was limited to a single instance, but I had heard some very terrifying accounts from other students. Even worse, they had enlisted

one or more sets of parents. I assumed they wouldn't care because we're all adults, but that wasn't the case.

My lips formed a sneer.

Neela, a friend of mine, was quite reticent when she related the conversation she had with her parents afterward.

And only two days later she was back at it with the booze. Possible that she still hadn't learned her lesson...

I said, "Why are you grinning like that?"

In an instant, my attention was drawn to Cade, who was standing off to the side and observing me. As he leaned against the wall, he looked toward the kitchen. Disarray surrounded his unkempt head of hair.

I shook my head and faced him once again. Until now, he had waited. "It doesn't amount to anything."

He squinted at me as he cocked his head sideways. Before he moved away, we locked gazes for a split second. I can't pick this lock, he said.

He tried pulling on the door handle, but it was stuck. After discovering food was being stolen, they upgraded to this more sophisticated model.

I let out a loud snort. Did you do that?"

After a moment of silence, his eyebrows arched upward, and he peered across at me. "Are you underestimating me?"

I didn't say anything and forced myself to grin.

He shook his head in exasperation, his back once again turned away from me. At least that wasn't me, he thought to himself.

I burst out laughing. It surprised me when he admitted it. He obviously did not give a hoot about what other people thought of him. For some reason, it appealed to me.

He wasn't going to be the kind of man who lied about everything to maintain his good name.

What are our next steps, then? I inquired, arms crossed. Felt like I was going to freeze to death. I should have considered wearing a sweatshirt underneath my coat. It was too late now, however.

Cade scanned the area. He kept staring fixedly through the little window in the wall of the kitchen, at the area where the food was distributed. He turned to me and said, "I think you could get through."

My irises sprung open. “What?”

"The blinds in the lunchroom where the women hand out food won't open for me. However, I'm certain I could get the window open.

The man grinned at me and his message. I'm willing to wager that you're a manageable size to squeeze through the door.

As my heart rate increased, I became anxious.

Was he trying to fool me?

With a grin on my face, I spoke out. Aren't there any alarms set up in there?"

Cade had already started towards the glass.

“Cade?”

He fumbled with the window and began to fiddle. When you looked at it closely, you could see it wasn't glass but rather thick plastic. The window was built using a sliding mechanism, which I was aware of. A little lock was attached to its side.

Is it likely they'd spend money on alarms?

I raised an eyebrow and nodded my head. I shifted my stance such that my arms were crossed over my stomach and the torch was resting on my hip. Certainly, Cade. If I hadn't wanted to know, why would I have asked?

His sigh was audible. Can I borrow a pin or something?" What do the females do in their hair to make it seem so good?

I responded with a nod and a hand to my bun, saying, "Bobby-pins." I took out a safety pin and approached him.

“Here.” I extended my hand and he took it. The reason I was still aiding him was unclear at this time.

I was afraid that if I entered, I may accidentally trigger an alarm.

“Thanks.”

He fiddled with the lock by twisting the bobby pin. I was trying to make sense of what he was up to, so I kept a careful eye on him. Even though I had seen it done in movies, I had never given it a try.

For some reason, I brought my hand up to my face and began chewing on my fingernails. It was completely out of my control. To which the respondent must ask, "Do you honestly think-"

Let me go closer to the lock for a second, he mumbled. He worked the bobby pin around inside it carefully, and after a few seconds, it was secure. A note of victory escaped his lips as he yanked the lock open and dropped it to the floor.

He grinned and said, "Told you I could do it." When he looked at me with that devilish glint in his eye, I recoiled.

“No.”

His face lit up with a wide smile. We've reached the point when it's your turn, Holly.

"Cade, I-"

To get me in front of the glass, he grabbed my left hand and drew me forward. Holly, it's not that complicated. Please come in and unlock the door. Please wait for me.

I yanked on my own hand. I swear to God! Seriously, where did he get that idea?

Have I ever mentioned my phobia of the night? Well, if not, I'll tell you this:

Confused, Cade shook his head. I'll get my cell phone and turn on the lights, Holly. Nothing will happen, I swear to you.

Astonished: "How could you even know that?"

For a brief moment, we locked gazes. Instinctively, I made a fist with my hand.

As time went by, he still hadn't responded.

"Is that all there is?" To put it mildly, I was hesitant in asking. That's something I'd only agree to if absolutely nothing else was possible.

The answer is "No," since there is none.

That's when I forced myself to swallow my anxiety. One might feel a bump.

in my pharynx I groaned and shook my head, saying, "Alright."

Already, I was beginning to feel remorse.

However, at this time, all I wanted was to cat. Plus, I was probably going crazy from hunger.

What are our plans for achieving this?

His lips curled into a devilish grin. When prompted with "I could-"

Quickly, I lifted my light and pushed my palm on his lips. You can't convince me with that glare, Mister. If you keep talking like that, I'll have to smack you.

Under my fingers, his smile grew, and one of his eyebrows raised.

My head trembled, and I turned to give him the cold shoulder.

The chairs and tables were all there. After a little pause, inspiration struck. "Let me have a seat."

When I finally let go, I thrust the torch into his hands. I redirected my attention to the closest table and moved over to pull up a chair on top of it. I staggered over to the pane of glass and shot Cade another look. Don't stare at me like that," he joked.

Almost in a snarl, I directed my anger at him. What the heck, I'll go ahead and look around. I think you're simply trying to deceive me. I will kill you in every way I can.

I positioned the chair in front of the glass and climbed up upon it. I raised my trembling hands to the wall in an effort to stabilize myself. I swung my head around to see what was going on behind me.

As soon as Cade caught my sight, he looked up at me. I shot him a snarky message that said, "Where's my light?"

He walked up to me and shone the light into the kitchen so that I could see better. My head trembled and I closed my eyes and took a few long breaths.

No, I wasn't imagining anything.

Plus, I wanted it to be clear that Cade was to blame for any misfortune that occurred.

To hell with this.
After getting my feet inside, I squished my upper body in. When I stumbled and let out a puff, it seemed like I was standing in the air. I yelled and crashed to the ground, falling hard on my hands and knees.

"Holly?!"

It caused a moan for me. "Fuck!"

How are you doing? Cade voiced his question emphatically.

My eyeballs rolled. I wasn't. My hands and legs were in excruciating pain, and I couldn't move. Following this, I'll need some space to gather my thoughts.

Assuredly, Cade. No, I'm perfectly alright. Never felt this good.

Four

Cade's illuminating the room with his flashlight was completely ineffective. As I got to my feet, I moaned about how much my knees hurt. I got in here without giving any attention to what might happen next.

I don't know why I assumed I'd be able to immediately get up.

Physical education was never my strong suit. I was only good in sports that required me to toss or kick a ball. They gave me a chance to vent some of my repressed anger. And it felt great to hurl these projectiles at those I disliked.

The urge to lob a ball at Cade seemed overwhelming at the moment.

I'd grab it without a second's hesitation if I came across one amid all this chaos.

In a way, he was responsible for my getting here...

“Holly?” Once again, his voice echoed across the air.

It had a deep, dumb voice.

“Yes?” I asked, out of breath. I gently tucked the stray hairs behind my ear where they belonged when they escaped my bun. I was a total wreck. The pain in my hands felt like they were on fire, and my knees were aching.

One could only hope that everything would settle down shortly.

When will you be arriving?

I let out a sigh of exasperation.
Just how quickly did he want me to get up after that?

I forced myself to control my frustration and made a forward movement. I couldn't see where my hip was going and accidentally hit something. The metal was clanking and I felt my chest tighten. The answer is, "I'm trying, Cade."

I looked around to see how much damage I had done, but it was too dark. Hold the torch correctly, you damn fools! "I can hardly make out anything in this fog.

The problem was fixed by his alterations.

It took a while, but I finally started to see the details. Close by, on a metal table, were a few metal containers and glasses. Thankfully, nothing except the metal had shifted. Cleaning up the shattered glass in the dark would have been difficult.

When can we expect results?

"Just-" My left knee was killing me, and I had to clench my teeth through the agony. My chest tightened as I sputtered for air. When I looked at myself, I realized I'd done a number on myself. "Stop babbling already."

The kitchen door was visible to my left as I peered around. I took a deep breath and set off on foot. I needed to go back to my room right about now. It seemed like a wonderful plan to just stay in bed, sip some tea, and read a good book.
The phrase "oh well" escaped my lips. I had to start by getting some sustenance.

My hand sprang out, and my fingertips just barely touched the door. My mouth began to form a grin. One thing I had done correctly, at least.

I put out a hand and grabbed the door knob. Totally still. It was just how I had anticipated. In an offhand way, I shook my head and chewed my lower lip. I'll be right outside. I'm at a loss; what must I do now?

Cade nailed it with his response, "Just open it."

It was at this point that I rolled my eyes and huffed. Cade, I'm not sure if-"

Simply flip the clasp to open.

I froze and lowered my gaze. Indeed, there it was. All of a sudden, everything looked simple... And you have the audacity to claim that you can't get this open?

His humor was evident in the sound it made. In other words, "I could've. I was curious as to how far you would go.

My blood was boiling and my heart was racing. My fist tightened around the doorknob, and I gritted my teeth. Damn that scumbag. Where does he get his arrogance?
I took a big, deep gulp of air.

Without a word, I reached for the latch and turned it, then waited for him to arrive. As soon as I pushed in the door, the light from behind me vanished. His every stride was audible to me.

He walked right up to me, that same idiot grin on his face.

It was then that I licked my lips. That angered me to the f*cking max.

As I walked away from him, I shook my head. I jumped as the light went on behind me as he pursued me. My eyes widened as I returned his gaze. I had not seen the light switch that was so conveniently located next to the entrance.

With a groan, I re-circled back toward the storage units. They lined the wall across from the entrance.

Against the stark white of the wall tiles, the green had faded and appeared aged. Grey wall cabinets were mounted above them, and I had a sinking feeling that I would never be able to access the items stored there.

You may have the wall cabinets. I'll have a look inside the cupboards.

With a yelp of pain, I got on my knees and opened the first door. Great. Nothing. So I squirmed my way to the next one, where I discovered a meager selection of canned soup and crackers. I retrieved them and put them in storage containers.

Cade was right there by me, but all I could hear were the doors slamming and opening.

Nothing seemed to have changed in his situation.

But I've decided to pay him no mind. Even though I wasn't in danger thanks to my companions, I still couldn't make out his face. Those scrapes on my knees wouldn't exist if it weren't for him.

The next thing I knew, I heard his little chuckle. While searching, I came across marshmallows and cocoa powder.

That's when I let out a moan. Why are you being so kind to me?

The next shelf over had various-sized cheese containers. To express my discomfort, I grimaced. I'd sooner starve to death than eat it if it's our last hope of survival. The cheese was always something I avoided. Without touching them, I put the cabinet door back on.

Next to my stuff, he put the things he'd discovered. I proceeded to the subsequent storage unit. Nothing, once again. It was quite annoying.

Cade shifted positions and was now standing behind me. To his credit, he still managed to go to the storage areas. There was close contact between his shins and my side. The muscles in my shoulder blades tightened. For what reason did he have to empty every cupboard save the one directly above me? Nothing required physical contact on our part.

Not after he lied to me, anyhow.

More loudly than I would have liked, I slammed the door.

I said, "Are you mad at me?" Cade probed, and I felt his eyes on me. I took a big, deep gulp of air.

To ask, "What do you think?"

We waited silently for a whole second.

His only justification was that he didn't imagine you'd really do it.

Reacting with "Oh?" After rolling my eyes, I squirmed to the side to get some distance. On the other hand, he wouldn't allow me. I had to step around his legs as he stepped to the side. With a sigh, I let myself slump backward, collapsing on my butt. Forcing myself to do so, I flexed my legs out in front of me and grimaced as the pressure on my knees increased.

Angry and defiant, I refused to meet his gaze and instead focused my attention on his knees. I'm sure I looked like a toddler having a temper tantrum, but I didn't care. For the time being, at least, I identified with that category.

I didn't want you to injure yourself," she said. To Holly, I apologize.

To put it simply, I gulped.

To be honest, I didn't think he'd bother to apologize. Perhaps he wasn't quite the sexist pig I had made him out to be... True, but even so. I leaned back, palms flat on the earth. I raised my eyes to meet his. Their eyes locked with me, he wore a frown.

I don't apologize to anybody, so you'll just have to accept it. He smiled briefly and extended his hand to me. There, he waited.

Before acting, I waited a few seconds.
I hoped he wouldn't take it as normal, however. If he kept treating me the way he was treating you, I wouldn't stand for it.

I heaved a sigh, shook my head, and gave in. Getting into a fight right now wouldn't solve anything. We'd be stuck together for the next several days.

"Fine, but don't think you're off the hook," I said. He pushed me up onto my feet. We took a look at the data we had gathered. Some crackers, some marshmallows, some cocoa powder, and a couple of cans of soup and veggies... What wonderful news. The chances of survival are low.

"Why are there marshmallows in this?"

To this, Cade just shrugged. Obviously, you'll need them to get into the holiday mood if we're going to be here for Christmas.

A frown formed between my brows and I cast a glance in his direction. Enjoy the spirit with marshmallows? In what kind of a parallel universe do you exist?

He made a joking motion and put his left arm over my shoulders, drawing me to his side. My lungs felt like they were emptying. Actually, it was the last thing I was expecting. Holly, you'll see," he said with a grin.

Five

I said, "Mom," and then I burst into a hearty chuckle. I tried to determine whether my impaired vision was due to fatigue or if I genuinely required glasses as I stared at her hazy figure. So that I could see her better, I squinted. "I bet you have no idea what I was dreaming about."

My line of sight was obstructed by her plan when she shifted.

My chest tightened as I sputtered for air. There was a general haze across the whole scene. A snowstorm kept me inside my dorm room all day.

No one said anything in response; it was dead silent. I frowned thoughtfully.

"Mom?" The sound of my voice reverberated in my skull. I scowled and glanced around, but saw nobody there. I was in my normal squalor of a bedroom at home. The problem was that everything seemed hazy.

"Mom?"

It was a clumsy stride forward, but I made it. My vision dilated and a cry from my lips as I prepared to plummet to the earth.

My whole body sprang forward, and I gasped while clinging to my comforter. The brightness of my surroundings caused my eyes to water, so I hid my head behind the curtain. I closed my eyes and took a deep whiff of my laundry detergent—the cheap one I only use for school.

When I finally opened my eyes, I found myself staring at the ceiling. The constellations on it always seemed to me to be represented by the little specks. Shakily, I let out a breath. I was away from my residence. Without a care in the world, I sat up as the earth began to rumble.

My eyes were instantly drawn to the windows.

Were you able to tell whether it was still snowing? The sunshine was shining in through my white curtain, but I couldn't see anything. In other words, they were not transparent.

Gradually, I threw off the comfort of the blanket and got to my feet. After a brief pause, I made my way to the window and pulled back the drapes. The snowfall had not stopped. The white slop was smeared all over campus, effectively eliminating any semblance of color.

To calm myself, I sat down and pressed my palm on the chilly window. It felt like ice under my feet. I tucked them in and sat down. My hands were trembling.
My head cocked to one side. It was quite unusual to see the campus deserted since it generally bustled with activity regardless of the hour. As much as I've always hated the constant noise, I'm beginning to want a little peace.

As a result, I let out a heavy sigh.

Nothing I did could make the snow stop, yet it kept falling nonetheless. This was nature's way of torturing me. Perhaps this was the result of karma... That's why I was dreading returning home to Arthur.

This year, though, I would be spending Christmas without her.

In all of human history, it had never occurred.

I had always made it a point to get there at least five days early, even before her recent marriage. She would always wait for me to put up the tree and make the cookies for the holidays. They wore that silly Santa hat to welcome me when I arrived.

Although at the time I had rolled my eyes at her, I was beginning to miss it. I needed to talk to her.

For some reason, I shook my head. My forehead wrinkled as something moist poured down my face. A tear formed, and I raised a hand to my face to wipe it away. As I watched it trickle down my finger and into my palm, I took a big breath.

When I saw what was happening, I squeezed my hand into a fist.

I was a complete and utter wuss. My eyes closed for an instant as I wiped my cheeks with my palms after a round of sniffling. I took a few full breaths in. This had to end immediately. As a coward, I had to quit being one.

I was 19, so I was officially out of the "child" category.

I was stuck dealing with the consequences of my own actions.

When a ringing echoed across the space, I drew back in fear. After a moment, I swung around.

My alarm clock looked like this. Have I overlooked something? In order to get my phone from the nightstand, I circled the bed. When I saw the time, my pupils dilate.

The time was 8:30.

Cade and I had agreed to see each other at eight in the morning.

I panicked when my phone almost fell off my bed and ran to my dresser. The doors were flung open by me. What I have on are a sweatshirt and some pants, and they'll have to do.

I put on a new outfit and ruffled my hair. That was beyond my capabilities, and I just did not have the time to address it. The first thing I did this morning was sit down on my bed and put on my socks and shoes. I didn't care about my appearance at all. Cade was now the one who had to deal with this.

I got out of bed and fumbled for my phone. Just fifteen minutes had gone by. Good.

He probably hadn't gone yet, and if he had, he wouldn't have gotten very far. We were trapped inside and had no way out.

In any case, I was eager to learn the answer immediately. I fell down and had to quickly get my wits about me. My knees twinged with agony as I walked to the door, but I paid it no mind. When I went back to my room late last night, I took my first look at the bruises.

Unfortunately, I was too exhausted to care.
As soon as my head struck the pillow, I closed my eyes. Yet, unhappily, I had awakened twice throughout the night... There was a guy with a knife following me around campus in my dream.

What I had created in my head out of my apprehensions was beautiful.

When I woke up yesterday, I was certain that I was going to die. Even though Cade had laughed at me, there was absolutely no humor in what had happened. My eyeballs rolled. This guy lacked basic social graces.

As I left, I made sure to secure the door behind me. As things were, I had to get going. I was always so upset with myself when I was late or broke a commitment. Why hadn't I woken up sooner? In the past, I've gotten up every morning at six o'clock...

It was impossible for me to alter my bedtime routine. As long as I had to get up early, my internal clock worked well, but I could never sleep in. There was a consensus among my circle of friends that I was completely bonkers.

It was humiliating that I was usually the one to sleep in first whenever we stayed at one another's places. As I lay there like a drunk, I could hear them conversing. My cheeks started to flush as a smile formed on my lips.
I was unable to resist.
Having turned a corner, I walked while dragging my hand along the walls. Nobody spoke; the atmosphere was eerily silent. The unusual silence made the situation seem weird. I glanced to the side and saw that the snow was becoming much heavier. There wasn't as much of a brisk breeze, but the sky was a thick sheet of white.

We're down to only two days till Christmas!

My lower lip went into my mouth. That we could have escaped this place sooner was never a wish of mine. A year of alone in my chamber would be the norm if nothing changed. But if I could only get some liquor, maybe things wouldn't be so horrible...

I'll have to check and see if we have any leftovers. Neela had informed me that we ran out, and all I could do was hope that she had refilled. Without it, I wasn't sure how long I'd be able to keep going.

Who knew I'd have to suspect the worst of Cade? What he did yesterday may have been the start of something far more serious. I avoided finding out what would occur since I didn't care. He would most likely do anything that would result in my death.

After that, I went down a hall. All that remained was for me to enter through the massive doors at its far end. I would have to look for Cade if he wasn't present.
It was one of those days when I just felt so damn unmotivated.

As I moaned, I grabbed the door handle and yanked it open. I went in there and had a look around. No one else seemed to be in the hall. As I looked around, my eyes lingered on the stone walls, the cozy fireplace, and the comfortable sofas. To make out what was going on, I narrowed my pupils.

Had he-

No, he still had his legs and shoes. I frowned thoughtfully.

As seen from above, he had flipped over on one of the sofas and was hanging upside down. Its rear was entirely hidden from my view. I stumbled and tried not to burst out laughing. I don't know what he was thinking.

My lips started to pull into a grin. I gave a little shake of my head and walked up to him.

I was curious as to the context of this discussion.

There was a constant bouncing of his foot. When I could, I avoided making any noise. I didn't want him to stop doing whatever it was he was doing.
Like he had done to me the day before, I silently approached him. I was standing next to his legs and peered down at him, where I saw that he had his eyes closed. I cracked a happy smile. His head was bobbing and his fists were tapping the air to a beat that only he could hear.

That's when I finally yelled, "What the heck are you doing?"

Six

As he flinched, his eyes widened in surprise. If I hadn't grabbed his leg, he surely would have fallen off the sofa. I burst out laughing uncontrollably.

The noise resounded throughout the building.

He yelled, "Fuck, Holly!" as he sat up. When I had him sit up, his butt was still on the sofa and his other leg brushed my hip. When I looked down at him, I couldn't help but laugh. Get what you deserve, you jerk, I thought.

To steady himself, he grabbed the sofa's back. His eyes were wide as he sat there, his legs propped up on the back of the chair.

What the fuck?" he gasped. He looked at me in total and complete amazement. After that, I gave a little smile.

"Why did you do that?"

For an instant, a furrow formed between his brows. Next, redness appeared on his cheeks. His cheeks were truly red.

I squeaked out, "Aw, how sweet."

My right hand went out to touch him on the head. Do you need me to hold your hand as Pour Cade Thindal did?

As I tried to pull away, he grabbed my hand. The idiotic smile that had been on his lips was now on top of mine.

Saying, "That's not humorous! I could've fallen and broken my neck!"

After holding back my laughing for a while, I was ready to let it all out. As much as I tried to cover my lips with my hand, it was too late. I let out a great big snort of laughter.

It takes me at most a minute to macro-mode myself.

With a smile still on my face, I locked eyes with Cade.

A smile of his own was something he had to suppress. "Okay... I guess that was kind of hilarious... And to answer your question: yes, I was waiting for you!

After a moment, I cocked my head to one side. Oh, so that's what you've been up to all this time? Then why were you pounding about in the air?"

I can't think of any instance where it happened.
I gave a chuckle and a smile at him. The grin on his face had returned.

My head trembled. What a little man he was.

He made an effort to yank his calf back. When I checked my hands, I realized I still had it in my possession.

My face flushed and I said, "Oh, sorry."

Not until now did I realize that I was almost wedged between his legs. My left hand was holding the opposite leg while his left was at my right hip. When I let off, he turned around and got to his feet. The sofa had been moved to provide space between us.

As he walked around the sofa, he finally questioned, "What took you so long?" He leaned his hip on his folded arms. I raised my eyes to his and licked my lips.

My hands fiddled with the cuffs of my sleeves as I said, "I overslept." Suddenly, my heart rate increased.

Not knowing whether or not it was due to him, I couldn't say for sure. My anxiety would strike at odd intervals. Still, I couldn't say for certain that it was the case. It felt like my heart was racing. To maintain my footing, I tightly clutched the sofa.

It seems like Cade could sense my distress. Are you feeling okay?

I took a step back, nodded, and swallowed. I smoothed my left-side hair behind my ear. Have you eaten anything yet?

He arched a shady brow in my direction, but he eventually stopped. I was expecting you to ask me out on our first date, Holly," he joked, regaining his wry grin. His grin spread like wildfire. "Let's go eat some breakfast together."

At one of the cafeteria tables, I found myself. Cade was found cooking. He instructed me to take a seat while he made dinner. There weren't many choices, so I figured he was probably just rewarming some soup in the microwave.

I wasn't sure if I could put my faith in him and whether he could truly utilize it.

After a while, I relaxed completely in my seat. Everything seemed normal once again now that the lights were on. For the time being, at least, I had overcome my fear.

The fact that I felt at ease in Cade's company was significant. The vast majority of males were so self-absorbed that I couldn't bear to be around them for more than five minutes. Without a doubt, Cade had the potential to be rather irritating.

On the plus side, he wasn't behaving like them. When it came to his personal life, he appeared quite reticent... but I digress. Yesterday was the first day we began conversing.

Cade flung open the kitchen door. When it slammed up into the wall, it startled me. Maybe this put a dent in things...

My eyes widened as he walked by holding two plates, but he didn't stop or say anything. He cracked a grin at one point. A fool, that's what he was. I got to my feet and brushed by him on my way to look at the wall.

I certainly wouldn't want to foot the bill for anything so ridiculous. There was no need to inquire; I had not entered this chamber. The sight of the wall made me wince, so I closed the door quickly. It was hard to overlook the ding. As I bit my lip, I ran my fingers over the rough wallpaper.

Soon after touching the augmented wall, my fingers naturally curled into the nooks and crannies. Over my shoulder, I saw Cade setting the table.
N “Hey!”

When he caught sight of my face, he glanced over his shoulder and chuckled. "Holly, you can't give me that look. Stop ruining everyone's good time.

"I let out a huff. To paraphrase, "You smashed through the glass, Cade!"

After chuckling, he cocked an eyebrow. "'Broke the wall?' Honey, I don't believe you've ever seen devastation before! That's hardly even a scrape.

I scowled and folded my arms over my chest. Scratch my arse," etc. No, you haven't even bothered to look at it, you moron!

To which she said, "Oh, we're already that far in our relationship? "I always assumed pet names were only necessary after the second date..."

It took me a second to register his presence, so I blinked. Seconds later, I moaned and threw my hands up in disgust. I had no intention of telling him about this. Okay, OK... but if we get in trouble, you'll have to foot the bill for the repairs.

He chuckled and said, "Fine with me."

He just didn't give a damn. So I began to speculate whether or not he ever has genuine anxiety about issues of this kind. After dropping Taylor's phone a few weeks ago, I nearly sobbed when I saw the fresh crack in it.

Yet, each individual was unique. Moreover, I was aware that I was sometimes extremely sensitive to certain stimuli. The very thought of it made me cringe; it was one of my many flaws.

Cade plonked himself down and patted the empty seat next to him. The speaker said, "Holly, please come here. The question is, "You wouldn't want to miss our date, would you?"

With a grunt, I walked up to him. "No way, Cade!" I tried to present my best self for the occasion! No, of course, I hadn't thought of it. As I ran late, I didn't even bother to glance in the mirror once I got up.

There was no way he couldn't tell.

He smiled and said, "You're always lovely to me." The twinkle in his eye suggested something was up. You have no idea how long I've been waiting to do this," he said with a wry grin.

I cracked a grin at him. We both had a gut feeling he was making it up. The nervousness in my tummy was unwarranted. Truth be told, I had never heard of the person before.

I joined him at the table and took a seat in front of the hot serving dishes. A tan fluid filled them up. I cast my gaze toward Cade. Finally, "So, what have you arranged for us?"

He smiled as he sat back in his chair. You can see that I've made us some delicious chicken soup. Softly removed off the shelf by my deft hands.

Ugh, I sighed. If I had to guess, I'd say, "You've probably spat in mine now..."

To which the respondent must ask, "Who do you believe I am?"

I twisted my head and raised an eyebrow at him. There was no way I could keep from smiling. Does it really matter if you do?

He blinked at me narrowly and leaned in closer. When we were face to face, I could feel his breath on my cheek and on my chest. Suddenly, I could make out the glint of gold in his otherwise dark brown eyes. They made me think of the universe.

There was no way for me to Until now, he had escaped my attention.

He said, "I want to know so much." Simply said, "Everything, Holly. Please fill me in on every little detail.

Seven

I stared out the window as I brought my spoon to my lips. The snowfall continued unabatedly... Just the thought of that gave me the creeps.

The snowfall was the first time in my life that I was caught in one. So far, the worst event I've experienced was a moderate earthquake in my own country. To be honest, I hadn't even noticed it before. I fell asleep in my room and heard about it on the news when I woke up.

It had been as unbelievable as it is right now.

The hot soup went down easy. The absence of bread and toast was disappointing. I've never before had such tasteless soup, but that was our only option. Those were difficult times, and I had to take drastic action... but now I'm just being theatrical.

When I turned to look at Cade, I saw that he, too, was intently studying the snow. He wrinkled his nose in disgust, and I smiled despite myself. We nearly found his naiveté endearing.

"When do you expect it to end?" This was an unexpected question from Cade.

I frowned thoughtfully.

Honestly, I didn't even think he'd seen me gazing. It seemed as though he were on another planet. My first assumptions, however, seemed to be incorrect. “What?” That's what I was wondering, anyhow. In that little time, I had already forgotten all he had spoken.

How long do you think it will be until the snow stops falling? He grinned and shot me a glance. He seemed to be having a good time.

I took a deep breath and turned back to the window. It seemed like the snowfall would never end. I said hesitatingly, "I'm not sure."

In case I was wrong, I didn't want to offer him any reason to hope against reason. What a nasty and inhumane thing to do. As much as I wanted to see my own family, I'm sure he felt the same way about his.

I'm crossing my fingers we can get out of here before Christmas, but I hear the news reports aren't looking good.

He leaned back and licked his lips. He abandoned his half-eaten bowl of soup and the spoon on the dish.

He no longer seemed interested in eating. He was holding his arms across his body.

"Would it be that horrible if you spent Christmas with me?"

Instantly, I creased my brows in thought.

Was he really thinking about it?

I met his gaze and responded, "I suppose it wouldn't be that horrible." A new kind of glimmer caught my eye.

There was ambiguity around his emotions that I was unable to decipher. "But you must miss your loved ones, right? Imagine a holiday season without them!

There was a hearty laugh, and he put his hand to his lips. When he grinned, you could see every one of his pearly whites. Invariably, I do, Holly. However, I see your point. As a child, celebrating Christmas with my family was the highlight of my year.

I sucked in my lower lip.

I didn't miss the fact that he was speaking in the past tense. Was there a problem? When I started to speak, he had already pushed back in his chair and got up.

He lifted his plate and said, "I'll simply bring it back." As he moved away from me, he didn't so much as a glance in my direction. I did the same, my palm resting on the chair's back as I watched him stoically make his way to the kitchen. I promise to be right back.

My silence and shock left me speechless. What to say or do, I had no idea. Either way, I would have been limited to talking to myself if I had been aware. He simply abandoned me at this spot. The only thing I could do was keep stuffing my face.

Once he was out of sight, I heard the door to the kitchen slam shut behind him. My neck sagged and my shoulders drooped.

After a moment of fixation on the wood, I sighed and returned my attention to the table. As I refocused my attention on my plate, I retracted my spoon. I kept on chewing. Everything now had an unsettling, unfamiliar flavor on my tongue. The soup tasted much worse than it normally does. I had no idea what was going on or what had just occurred to me.

What if I had really said something? They glued themselves to my brain till I couldn't help but analyze every possible outcome. Do you think he had a problem with me?

Maybe he simply wanted to go home and was upset because he couldn't find his ride, but that didn't seem likely. I had a strong suspicion that he wanted to flee the situation as much as I had, but it didn't seem to be the solution to the mystery.

This could only be related to my actions.

After a long sigh, I plopped my elbow on the table and buried my chin in my palm. When some of the liquid splashed upon me, I reluctantly let the spoon go back into the dish. Putting my left hand over my face, I closed my eyes. I've always had a knack for messing up.

For some reason that I could never quite pin down, I often found myself inadvertently saying really insensitive things when they were most inopportune. There were instances when I talked before I'd had a chance to consider my words. My lips seemed to pour out words like a river...

My apologies are in order.

I didn't want him to have any unfavorable feelings about me, so I tried to avoid whatever it was.

In the end, I blinked my eyes open once again. The tension in my body manifested as a tightening of my shoulders and a general uncomfortably. My fingers ran over my hair and I turned back to the kitchen.

Exactly when would he be returning?

Exhaling deeply, I sighed.

Then again, maybe I should go find him. The food once again caught my eye. Even if I wasn't pleased, there wasn't much left. My chair was pushed back, and I cautiously rose, being as quiet as possible.

After turning around and picking up my plate, I said. I'm hoping this isn't a terrible plan. Despite the horrific consequences I foresaw, at least I was making an effort. Surely it meant something, right? That was something I wasn't entirely certain about, but it wouldn't stop me now.

Without a solution, I would have to bear the repercussions for the next several days. You couldn't get around each other very easily. Certainly, we each had the option of locking ourselves in our bedrooms, but it would serve no purpose.

In all likelihood, if I remained in my room for more than a day or two, I would begin to feel depressed.

Exhaling deeply, I sighed. Why didn't things work out as we expected?

If everything had gone as planned, I would be in my bedroom right now. The most that could happen is that I would be listening to mom and Arthur's dispute, but at least I would have been where I should have been.

Things were already messed up at home. Not much could be done about it, even with my presence.

Back at my place of residence, I was free to not give s***. That's true; I've been usurped by others. It was more convenient that way. For once, I didn't feel responsible for my actions since I could place the blame on someone else. Right now, though, there was just I. Not to mention Cade.

Every aspect of the situation was a complete and utter farce.

My attention fixed on the exit, I got up and began to walk. Not knowing what was going to happen, I took one foot in front of the other. In any case, I hope this goes quickly and ends soon.

Alternatively, it has the potential to ruin my mood for the remainder of my time in college. Unfortunately, the snow showed no signs of stopping.

I used one hand to hold the door open while the other held a bowl of soup in its place.

"Cade?" As I pushed open the door, I questioned. When our gazes locked, I froze in my tracks. Soup fell on the floor with a splash.

When he smiled at me, I frowned but still looked at him. Nothing had changed. Why did he seem to have moved on from this so quickly?

Want some, he inquired. He extended the marshmallows from the packet he was holding.

"Sure..." As I mumbled, It would be a lie to claim I wasn't confused. I took my plate over to the cupboards and set it there.

The soup had spilled on the floor, and I had to carefully avoid it. I didn't want to stink up my sneakers with it. When my hand became empty, I strolled up to Cade. As I popped one of the marshmallows into my mouth and observed his every motion, he took a step forward.

I looked up to see him gazing at my cheeks as I chewed. He was behaving strangely. Despite his best efforts to pretend otherwise, I could see that something was on his mind.

I took a deep breath and leaned against the kitchen cupboards. “Is everything fine? I'm sorry if anything is going on.

He nodded and reached for another marshmallow, which he promptly swallowed. As I looked, I found myself fixating on his shoulder.

For my part, I sensed that something was off. It appeared, though, that I would never learn the answer.

Eight

Cade was all smiles and chuckles.

He set the box of marshmallows down on the kitchen counter. I saw him take a deep breath in and then exhale a sigh of relief. We both sensed that something was off. It's simply that no one was quite ready to accept it just yet.

After shaking my head, I crossed my arms in a defensive position. And I certainly wasn't going to coerce him into saying so. He didn't have to tell me anything if he didn't want to. This was just our second day of talking regularly.

Our next move: "What are we going to do?" I cocked my head to the side and inquired. After my hair had fallen into my eyes, I reached up to smooth it back behind my ear. It's possible that I gave off a rat-like appearance. Like a raccoon-attacked dumpster-diver straight out of the trash can, for example...

I wanted to be fibbing.

I was becoming so bored it was unreal. I was completely at a loss for ideas.

Deep in contemplation, Cade was looking at a spot over my head. He began gnawing on his lips, and I couldn't look away. After what seemed like an eternity, a smile finally formed on his face. I can't wait to show you what I've got."

He opened the door behind me, turned around, and walked back to me. A grin crossed his face as he said, "Come on, Holly."

I followed him, and as he held the door open for me, I whispered my gratitude. When he halted a few meters inside the cafeteria, I waited for him to lead since I had no idea where we were headed.

He advanced swiftly. When he went somewhere, I followed him immediately. Moreover, his pace was lightning-quick. As we left the café, I started to break into a near-jog.

We made a left turn. Lockers lined the hallways to the left and right, and classroom doors appeared every few feet.

I racked my brain for any clues as to our destination. To the point where I could recite practically any route around campus by memory. Continuing to the right, we arrived at our next turn. Is it possible that we were on our way to the fitness center?

A detour to the left would get us there, but Cade was leading me astray, so I kept heading straight. There were not many possibilities left.

It's possible that we'll be visiting the physics lab, the geography classroom, or perhaps the office of the principal. I was praying he wouldn't try to break in.

As we passed the building housing the physics classrooms, my heart began to race. We were down to two choices, and one of them had already been taken. All I could do was hope I was wrong.

I couldn't think of anything that Cade wouldn't do based on his track record.

“Cade?”

He shot me a glance before responding, "Yes?"

"What are our plans?" Every time he moved, my eyes followed the motion of the muscles on his back.

I caught an indistinct giggle from him. "Hold on a minute, Holly.

I gave him a sideways glance and kept on going. As of right now, I could only imagine the worst-case scenario.

Now I was on the verge of running.

I suppose I could blame the length of his legs, but I knew it was only because I moved more slowly than he did. Plus, I was being a slug and my knees are still bothering me. It was important for that reason as well. That's how severely crippled I was.

We even made it past the geography classroom's closed door. I looked at her with widening eyes. That confirmed our suspicions that we were on our way to see the principal. The door was on our right, and we approached it.

Lightly tugging at the back of his jumper, I caught his attention. “Cade...”

His laugh returned to my ears. You shouldn't worry; it won't be that terrible. Yes, I will."

The word "huff" escaped my lips. "Cade, you and I both know where your promises lead me."

A moment went by.

Laughing, he said, "Well." When he shrugged, I caught a glimpse of a smile on his face. "I have nothing to object about."

No way in hell could he do it. Why the hell was I still following him? There was no justification for my presence. Simply said, I was bored and decided to come here.

But if we were caught, it wouldn't be a good excuse. My poor mother would be very upset if she knew! Perhaps I will even get expelled from university! Dear God, I was about to-

Unfortunately, I bumped into Cade's back. “Ouch!” After my nose made contact with his back, I let out an exclamation. Suddenly, he halted his stroll. With a scowl and a firm palm on his back, I pushed him away from me. Nose rubbing: me.

He cocked an eyebrow at me and smiled as he looked at me. I need to know where Holly is. "You're too preoccupied with your ideas."

In response, I grimaced and shook my head. Another smile appeared on his face, and he cocked his head to one side. His black hair had fallen into his eyes, and he brushed it back with his fingers.

And once again, he flashed that grin and that twinkle. However, things weren't the same this time around. It seemed like he'd found his joy again. Could be my imagination running wild...

Cade retreated a few steps and slung an arm behind him. His smile was wide. Let's have some laughs, Holly. In these dull times, we could use it equally.

Once his hand contacted the door, he halted his progress.

I advanced by one step.

He walked up to the entrance and reached for the doorknob. The loud snap that echoed down the corridor as he yanked it higher made me wince.

“Cade!”

He yanked on the door, then pushed it back up and in. He leaned against it, and a split-second later he was tugging on it.

Suddenly, there was a click. That was when my mouth dropped to the floor.

"How the f*** did you..." "I..."

Cade returned my gaze, smirking at me stupidly. He unlocked the door by pulling on the handle. There was no way I could tear my eyes away.

He didn't seem to be using that entrance for the first time.

Just one more, Holly! It's not like we have all day.

When I remained still, he reached out and grabbed my hand. Our faces were touching. It was a hushed "Come on," he said. My eyes narrowed as I stared at him in what seemed like a challenge.

After a little pause, I let out a heavy sigh. After I had gone over this threshold, there would be no turning back.

All okay, I said softly. I nodded and allowed myself to be dragged inside the office. This is a terrible plan. Somehow, I had an innate sense that this was the case. Somehow, however, he could persuade me to act in the most irrational ways.

Cade turned around and walked away from me without holding my hand. Suddenly, I was shivering. As I peered around, I crossed my arms over my tummy.

Only once before had I set foot in here. One of our professors had discovered us inebriated in the restrooms. On the two armchairs in front of the dim desk, there were four of us, all females, laughing. It was probably a disaster, but fortunately, I blocked out much of it.

Why we were drinking in the restrooms is beyond me.

I probably couldn't recall it because of how hazy the memory was, so I had to make an educated estimate. Perhaps someone needed to use the restroom and the others cheerfully followed. It was obvious to me that our loudness was the main reason for our capture.

Through the aisles, we engaged in a spirited discussion. That was what everyone else seemed to recall, at least. When Neela told me what happened the following day, she was crying tears of laughter. The thought of crying had crossed my mind as well, but for an entirely different reason.

We had been on Mrs. Quinn's bad side for months.

As a result, our academic performance dropped. When I thought about it, I had to suppress a shiver. Before this, my mother had never been so upset with me. More than two hours passed while we were on the phone together.

It was entirely passive on my part to listen to her talk. I hadn't even attempted to dissuade her. Like Arthur had so elegantly phrased in the background, I had been a "fucking kid who doesn't know better than to mess shit up."

I still took his s**t back then. This time it was me who yelled back at him. I couldn't say whether or not that really helped, but it certainly lifted my spirits. When Cade sat down in the principal's chair, his feet found a comfortable spot on the desk with a reassuring squeak. In mid-step, I halted and arched an eyebrow at him. Did he really think I would believe that?

Come sit down, Holly," he said. The armchairs in front of me caught his eye, and he made a corresponding motion. The good times are just beginning.

Nine

I was attempting to decipher the principal's reading material by focusing on the bookcase behind Cade. There was a whole wall of books, and I do not doubt that Mrs. Sullivan has read each one of them. She was a lady like that.

She has been the epitome of cleanliness ever since I met her. Her straight nose, grey suit, and high heels made her seem even more put together.

To me, it seemed like only scholarly literature was shown. Ugh, how dull...

Cade sat down slightly to the side, drawing my attention back to him. His mouth formed a grin. "What else merely adds to the fun?" he queried.

In an off-center incline, I cocked my head to one side. There was a click that reverberated across the space. Cade straightened up again, bringing an object to his desk. An enormous bottle of wine. I could only look at it.

He laughed and responded to me, "A lot of booze." Right then, the expression on my face had to be priceless. I was completely at a loss for words.

I frowned thoughtfully.

The first thing that sprang to mind was, "Where did you acquire it?"

Mrs. Sullivan "has a stock of kind," we may say.

Suddenly, I found myself staring into his intense blue eyes.

You had to be kidding me.

He grinned broadly and ruffled his hair with one hand while fiddling with the bottle with the other. The dark red tag bobbed up and down with his pounding.

You didn't know that "she loves to drink and put on sad music whenever she has to mark specific people's tests?"

After a long silence, I finally said out. Cade relaxed farther into the chair, his expression one of assured smirks. I was taken aback by what he was saying. He had to be making it up. That's impossible for you to know."

The man grabbed the bottle and raised it to his lips. He inspected it by turning it around so the tag was facing him. It's not all bad, being a shy child. There

has been a lot of instructor chatter that I have overheard.
I folded my arms in front of my tummy and leaned forward.

It was unclear whether or not I should put my faith in him. If this turned out to be true, it would completely alter my opinion of the principal. It wasn't hard for me to see her following his advice.

I gave a little head shake and let out a giggle.

Alcohol seems like it may be a need for some of the graders at this university. I couldn't bear to think of the chaos that would ensue when individuals tried to read their papers. To be honest, I probably would as well if I were a teacher.

Cade began rocking the bottle side to side, making shoulder movements that mirrored the bottle. I couldn't help but laugh at his ludicrous expression.

We can't drink Mrs. Sullivan's Wine regardless of whether you're telling the truth or not.

It seemed as if he were pouting at me. I mean, why not, Holly?

"We-" After a few long breaths, I shook my head. I could feel the impending doom coursing through my

veins. To which she replies, "I... I don't truly know, but wouldn't she miss it?"
The man let out a snort.

I don't believe she'd mind at the moment. Holly, they have no idea we're here.

I took a few long breaths and glanced out the window.

It seemed like the snowfall had lessened, yet it was still falling. And then there were other choices to be made... did I want to become drunk? And Cade?

Strangely, I felt a smile forming on my face. Indeed, it was the correct response. Not even to myself, of course! As of now, no more.

Once my gaze returned to him, I saw that it was returned by his own. Even just a little bit, he turned up his lips.

"What is the key to unlocking this?"

At that, we exchanged grins.

Cade reached across the table and grabbed a pair of scissors a split second later. He set the bottle down, still grasping it in his left hand.

He lifted the scissors over the bottle and said, "You only take the scissor. He unfolded it, holding it with one blade pointed downward. He flashed a smile at me. And then ram it down the cork's throat. Unquestioningly, he carried out his instructions.

I saw him bring the bottle closer to him before beginning to twist the scissors and eventually the cork. There wasn't much time before it exploded.

This caused the liquid to rise to the surface and bubble. Suddenly, the pupils in my eyes became larger. The spread would be tremendous!

Cade swore and got to his feet, putting the bottle down. He yanked the cork and tossed the scissors down.

He got up from the table to look around, leaving a puddle on the floor. He reached out and attempted to push his palm against the slit, but to no avail.

I looked up at him with wide eyes.

My chair swiveled and I looked over to the garbage can beside the exit. I sped up to do it.

“Here!” Then, with an exclamation and holding it in my hands, I turned around.

He hurried up to me and put the bottle to my lips.

We both stood there while the last of the liquid poured out. As it abruptly ended, I couldn't help but laugh. It was then that Cade and I locked eyes. You could tell he was having a good time because of his smile.

Well," he groaned, surveying the wreckage he'd left behind. The floor and the desk were stained with crimson wine. His whole sweater had been soaked. "I think we have a fantastic foundation to build on."

I found myself looking at the bright ceiling above me. On the top of my lips was a cringe-worthy smile. For some reason, I simply kept going.

Exactly what did you say? My inner child was laughing. I reached up and brushed my hair to one side.

Grumbling, Cade brushed my hair out of his eyes.

Our upper bodies were nearby, but our feet were oriented in opposing directions.

When he inquired, "What's your favorite color?" I told him that blue was my favorite.

To make eye contact with him, I tilted my head to the side and licked my lips. He had been resting on his side and staring at me the whole time.
I could feel his gaze upon me. After glancing at his physique, I raised an eyebrow. The thing that wasn't there.

At what point did he once again remove his sweater?

"Holly?" He drew my focus back to his gaze.

I looked at him blankly before laughing.

You couldn't make out his face very well. For a better look, I narrowed my focus.

"Yeah?"

In my mind's eye, I distinctly remember seeing the beginnings of a grin grow on his face. I thought I did, however. This whole world became hazy. It's possible that I need glasses right now.

The back of his palm reached up and gently brushed my head.

I cracked a joke and grinned broadly. Those feelings of fuzziness persisted.

He said again, "I inquired about your favorite color." His grin was now visible to me. His smile was genuine, not one of his usual smiles and smirks. That was OK with him. In a word, yes.
Even I had a grin on my face. Now I felt like I couldn't go on any longer. What I really said was, "Sunset is my favorite color."

His eyes were slightly closed, but his grin remained. I was crossing my fingers that it would remain on his lips. "Is it your preferred hue?"

It was a resounding yes from me. It strained my neck to keep craning it to see him. I coughed and shifted uncomfortably on my side.

Cade regarded the scene with amusement. Someone says, "What are you doing?"

I rolled onto my side and tried to catch my breath, but nothing came out. The weight of my mind forced my head to tilt to one side, where it eventually landed on the floor. When it became too much, I sighed and squeezed my eyes shut. A split second later, I opened my eyes again and whispered, "I'm trying to see you better."

My gaze quickly swept across his features. Initially, I couldn't take my eyes off his lips, but eventually, I started paying more attention to other things. With a grin on my face, I ran my fingers up his cheekbones and nose. Your freckles are lovely.

When his face flushed as red as a tomato, I couldn't help but chuckle. On the other hand, I appreciated the hue. It was like seeing the sun go down and the night sky come up thereafter. A lot of his freckles appeared like the stars in the sky, far, far away.

Ten

It caused me to look up at Cade and chuckle. He'd sat back up and was now smiling down at me. He put the bottle to his lips and gulped down another swig.

The movement of his throat as he swallowed fascinated me.

I smiled and said, "Me, too!" as they offered us food. To speak, I cocked my head back.

A cough came from Cade. Were you sure?"

To show my agreement, I nodded at him.

He gave me a shrug, hiccupped, and then poured the remains of the bottle over my head.

When the liquid got into my mouth, I had to cough it back up again right away. Overflowing from my lips, it splattered over my chin and neck. After what seemed like an eternity of coughing, I slid to the side, clutching Cade's knee.

In other words, my clothing was damp.

He laughed in astonishment as he set the bottle down next to my head. The back of my head felt a touch from his palm. He chuckled, "Poor Holly."

Embarrassed, I buried my head between his knee and the floor and frowned at my brows. With the support of his knee, I coughed a few more times and got to my feet.

Is it the booze, or does it seem like the world is spinning around me?

Sadly, I think I'll never find out.

When I was settled in, Cade spread his legs apart so that I was seated in the middle.

I slapped his leg and said, "That was so not nice."

Snorting, he seized my hand to prevent more blows from me. He showed no signs of being shaken by the experience.

I felt myself being yanked forward by his strong grip.

When I squeaked and landed in his arms, he chuckled and rolled over onto his back. As I landed, I made contact with him. My gaze was lowered to his body while my hands remained firmly placed on his chest. I burst into fits of laughter that I tried to suppress.

Cade raised his hand with a grin on his face. He ran his fingers over the black hair behind my ear. Cade whispered, "You're so gorgeous." His thumb gently touched my face as his fingers wrapped around my cheek. Have I ever told you that?

Lazily smiling, I rolled my eyes. As I leaned my head to the side, I made eye contact with his hand. During winter, he was my source of comfort.

He looked directly at me and said, "I mean it, Holly." His face was flushed, and I wasn't sure whether it was the alcohol talking. You may not remember the first time we met, but I certainly do. You've been stunning to me ever since. We've been doing this right from the start."

"That's a fantastic lulled speech," I said with a chuckle.

I put my right hand on his shoulder and kissed his forehead as I knelt. I laughed briefly and then kissed him on the lips again.

The look in Cade's eyes changed.

I took another backward step and braced myself by resting my left hand on his chest. Things are kept on a global scale.

But Cade, you've been drinking. We drank too much.

"Holly..." he shook his head.

He put his hand on my face, so I scooped it up and gave it a tight squeeze. Then, holding it in both of my hands, I bent down and gently placed it on his chest while smiling up at him.

To each other, we gave blank expressions. I was completely speechless; there was nothing I could have said. My heart was racing at a rapid pace, and I knew it wouldn't slow down any time soon.

Perhaps this was the first sign of a heart attack. Or maybe I was simply smashed.

The furrow that appeared between his brows made me chuckle. He seemed very bewildered and foolish when he was pinned beneath me.

A moment of grief erupted, but it quickly evaporated like raindrops on a windshield.

With a moan, he sat up. It wasn't long until my hand was back on his heart.

We leaned forward and locked gazes for a few seconds.

He put his hands on my upper arms before I realized what was happening. The man attempted to get to his feet.

He chuckled and pulled me up with him, saying, "I've got a dumb idea." He could shift gears in an instant, and I found myself wishing I have the same ability.

Once again, Cade hurried to the office desk. Get in here!

As I approached him, I accidentally collided with him. Laughing, he brushed his hip into mine, sending me stumbling to the side. I made a feeble attempt at a growl.

A dog being run over by a vehicle is probably how I sounded.

I had to laugh at myself.

As I looked on, he began to struggle with the little black machine on the desk's left side, bringing the microphone with him. He made some adjustments, and then clicked a button. The light from the little bulb shifted to green.

He flashed a broad smile in my direction. With a hushed gesture toward the microphone, he said, "Lean forward." My brows knitted together, and I reluctantly followed his instructions. My fingers were resting on the table's edge.

Say something, it says.

For a little while, nothing could be heard.

I sent him an inquisitive grin with my curled lips. He was silent after that. With a shake of my head, I shifted my focus once again.

I nearly spoke into the microphone as I said, "I'm at a loss for words."

When my words resounded throughout the room, I jumped in surprise. The pupils in my eyes dilated.

My eyes returned to Cade.

To ask, "What the heck was that?" To put it simply, I laughed.

Something I said just now reverberated all around us. Incredibly unreal.

"That was the school's intercom system," he said, his words a little slurred.

He swiveled around and pointed above. His aim wasn't the greatest, but I knew he was aiming for the odd grey items on the wall. I frowned thoughtfully.

Speakers, I think they were called.

It didn't matter to me at all. I did a complete about-face. "That Cade is so stupid he doesn't even wear sweaters is beyond comprehension!"

He let out a snort. However, the fact was that he hadn't yet re-donn his sweater.

My volume has increased. The laughter just kept coming out of me. It resounded all around us, and I realized I sounded ridiculous. I sounded like a quacking duck on the verge of death, and that made me nervous.

It came out slowly, almost in a whine: "Oh, no..." I wasn't complaining; who does that? Not me.

The question, "What's up?" Cade snickered. Also, his words reverberated all around us.

I put my head in my hands and gave a little shake of the head. There was a whirlwind and everything began to spin. "I sound like a duck about to die!" The phrase echoed around the building, echoing with the frantic pace of the students.

To express the pain I was feeling, all I could do was sigh.

Cade drew me in for a bear embrace. My arms quickly curled around his midsection, and I gasped with delight as he began rocking us gently from side to side. The two days I spent with him seemed like a lifetime. Days are unrealistic, but weeks or months are not.

Not only was the globe whirling, but so was I.

He said softly, "You're not a duck," as he leaned up close to my ear. I laughed heartily and nuzzled his chest with a smile. He swung us around so that we whirled. We danced on, listening to music that no one else could hear.

Because of how much I was grinning, my cheeks started to ache.

"Is there a soundtrack available for that?"

After a moment of silence, Cade gazed deeply into my eyes. If that's what you want," he said with a grin. He asked the tabletop machine, "Do you have your phone?"

I felt my front and back pockets, patted them down, and then put on my pants. One moment there was nothing, and the next it was there.
I reached inside my pocket and handed it up. So he donned it. Next, he shot me a glance. "What, you don't use a password?"

I shook my head and laughed. I doubt that anybody would take that ancient item.

With a humming sound, he circled back around. The drawer beneath the desk was unlocked and he rummaged among the cables. After searching for a while, he finally located the correct one for my phone.

He then affixed the wire to the device. "What tune do you wish to hear?"

A shake of my head was in order. "Naw. Truth be told, I don't listen to music on there.

He let out a snort. "Alright."

An old song that my mom had downloaded onto my phone began playing a few seconds later. The familiar music resounded through the

speakers. I cracked a happy smile. It didn't appear to go with our dance and was too sluggish. Intimate social gatherings or leisurely dances might be more appropriate.

Cade turned around to me and put my phone on the desk. To demonstrate, he extended one arm. "My dear, are you ready?"

With a kind nod, I shook his hand. “Always.”

He drew me close to him. My right hand remained in his, but my left found its way to rest on his shoulder. We got up and began to spin around the room. I didn't believe we'd be able to pull off any of these traditional dances, but we managed.

We may as well have been dreaming.

A bell suddenly rang, and our conversation was cut short. A complete halt was made by us.

As I twisted in his arms and returned my gaze to my phone, my brows furrowed. I got a call from my mother. My eyes rolled as I made my way to the table.

I was hoping she wouldn't come in on us at that moment. Moreover, I had no interest in hearing her argue once again.

No, I shook my head, and I didn't want to talk. I wanted nothing more than to be in this moment with Cade.

Inquiringly, "Who was that?" he approached me. His brows wrinkled as he inspected my phone.

I tightened my grasp on the desk and put my phone back into flight mode. I re-laid it on the table. Just me and my mom.

You can find yourself wondering, "What's wrong with her career choice?"

For the second time, I shook my head. It's just that something always seems to go wrong when she calls. The thing is, I don't want her to ruin-"

"How could you whine when you have this lovely family?" The lines on his face deepened as rage filled him.

I cocked my head to one side. I'm at a loss for words: "What did you say?"

With a shake of his head, he took a forward step. Holly, you have a family. You were born to wonderful parents, so why do you always seem to be complaining? I don't know what's wrong with you.

I gave him a blank look. That sick feeling in the bottom of my stomach. As my volume increased, I spoke more forcefully. "Cade, my father has passed away. That hardly qualifies as a picture-perfect scene, would you say?

After that he was quiet, glancing at my phone before looking back up at me. I saw something beginning to develop in his eyes, but I stifled its expression. Tears welled up in my eyes, and I shook my head. I backpedaled to get some space from him.

What a complete moron you are. I then slammed the door behind me as I walked out of the room.

ELEVEN

My feet gave out under me as I made my way down the endless corridors. The barriers kept shifting, but I wasn't going to stop until I'd gained some distance from Cade. The devil knows who he thought he was.

I let out a sigh of exasperation. My escape was necessary at the time.

My destination was the main lobby of the university, where I planned to enter the campus. I needed to travel to the nearest bus terminal, and quickly. I wasn't sure whether the buses were still running, but it was certainly worth a shot. I needed to get out of there. I had to do it.

I turned to my left and peered out the window.

The snowfall was significantly lower than it had been previously. However, it was situated on a rather elevated surface. To be honest, I was hesitant to try walking through it. Aside from the pristine snow, I could see that it was stagged on the highest rooftops.

When he said that, I clenched my teeth and shook my head. Sure, why not? Surely it can't be that terrible, right?

A left turn finds me leaning against the wall for support as I try to retain my balance. Those feelings of steadiness did not last. Nothing stopped the forward momentum of the globe.

I had to pause in my travels since I had fallen. I closed my eyes and took a deep breath to combat the lightheadedness.

Things were whirling around wildly. The thought of vomiting made me feel sick.

With my right hand, I pushed my stomach firmly. I don't understand why this is happening now.

All of this was completely unnecessary. At first, all I wanted to do was have a good time; suddenly, all I wanted was to get away from it all. I hoped I didn't have this overwhelming sense of isolation. Just a few minutes ago, everything was OK.

Sighing, I blinked my eyes open once again. When I felt my hand tense as I slid it from my tummy to my side, I shifted my grip. The hand I was holding on the wall advanced a few inches to the left. I risked trying to go even farther.

The knot in my throat forced me to swallow. It was time for me to quit being such a wimp. Getting there wouldn't take too much time at all!

I shook my head and stepped forward, leaning against the wall for support. If we could do that, everything would be perfect right now. I wasn't sure whether I could get back up if I tripped and fell. Perhaps it was necessary to wait it out.

With a sigh, I gave up. There was just one more turn before I would have to go back through the entrances. That wouldn't take too much time. Perhaps I could even make it back home.

After stumbling for a few minutes, I finally made it to the double doors. Behind me, I pulled one open and growled as I let it down.

The door to the chamber that would grant me freedom was finally in sight. I cracked a happy grin. I ignored the little fireplace and continued. Even the sofa where Cade had been resting. As I stared at it, a pang of sadness crept into my chest. The grin gradually disappeared from my face. To me, it seemed as though he were still present.

I just had to shrug it off. What I needed to focus on was not this.

As I got closer to the door, I could see that it was made of wood and was rather dark.

It wasn't too far to walk to the bus stop. If there wasn't so much snow, I may be able to get there. In anticipation, I reached for the door handle.

In theory, I ought to be able to handle this.

As for me, I'd-

The door sprang open, and a blizzard pelted the inside. My feet gave out from under me, and I fell backward. My mouth dropped open in disbelief at what I had just seen. Outside, nothing but whiteness could be seen. It seemed like the snow was higher than I was. I was at a loss for words.

That's why it started snowing, all right.

Not a light dusting of snow that failed to settle. Nature was urging me to screw myself with this. I shook my head and recoiled farther.

It hit me like a punch to the face, the harsh truth. The pressure of my heart against my ribs was intense.

The situation was too overwhelming for me to continue. At that point, I had a demeaning mental image of myself. Not just wearing a sweatshirt and pants, either. I can't survive the cold if I tried.

And all of that before I had even gotten close to the bus terminal. This was common knowledge among us, including me. And I gritted my teeth in frustration. Dammit.

And there was nothing I could do about it. The elements seemed to be conspiring against me.

I made a little forward motion to shut the door. It didn't bother me that there was still snow on the carpet. Getting away was all I wanted to do. It took me many minutes and a lot of effort to finally get the lock to shut. Once I heard the click, I pushed my body firmly into the wood and breathed a sigh of relief.

With my hand still on the door, I took a backward step.

I shook my head and brushed my black hair out of my eyes. My chest felt like it was about to burst.

I cleared my throat and swiveled around. That being said, all I could do at this point was go back to my hotel. Nonetheless, I was hesitant to take the initiative. Where Cade was, I had no idea. What's more, I couldn't bear to look at his face just then.

Not after I just discovered we couldn't get out of here. Everything felt very authentic. Not until the

snow had melted would it be possible to go. Time would be needed.
I let out what sounded like an almost sob from my mouth. When my lips began to tremble, I put a palm on them. There was a stinging sensation in my eyes and I knew tears were coming. The opposite must be true. The tears welled up in my eyes, but I stifled them.

On the contrary, not in this location. anything else than this spot.

Cade would notice the impact he made on me if he came along.

"You have the ideal family on paper, and you have the nerve to whine?

”

Incredulous: "What the heck is wrong with you?

”

Nothing in my family was really fine, unfortunately. My dad had passed away. And barely a year after his passing, my mom chose to wed again. I gave a head shake and walked away.

It was time for me to get back to my room. The only thing I could say for sure was that.

It took me less time than I expected to get there. Although I had no idea how to get there.

Everything happened so quickly.

With a whiff, I made my way to bed. Simply put, I sought cover. I could wait it out here in this haven, maybe... That was a fantastic proposal, I agree.

I drew back the sheets and got some shut-eye. There was a rustling sound as I shifted about on the bed, and then I was wrapped up like a burrito in the sheets. The air and everything around me was frigid. My heater was no assistance at all.

Tears escaped my eyes and my lips. I clutched at my own center, arms tight.

The only indication that time had passed was the gradual darkening of my room. Not even the thought of adjusting or closing my blinds had crossed my mind. I even had my shoes on at the time!

Furthermore, I experienced some head pain. It all hurt like hell...

I really needed a friend or a family member to talk to. If only one of my pals could come, that would be great. Honestly, even my mom would be fine right now.

My mouth shook with another sob.

The emptiness in my chest was overwhelming. I suppose I am overreacting. Maybe I just wasn't.

I have no idea at this time.

He looked so angry. It was a mystery to me what had transpired. Did he feel envious? Sad? The choice was entirely up to him. It's ridiculous that I care.

However, it appeared that he now deeply regretted his words. His eyes were different now; I shook my head and blew my nose. I had no idea why I was reacting in such a way. He was essentially an alien. And I had no prior knowledge of him.

Possibly my inebriation played a role in this. Simply put, we drank too much. That was a new side of Cade that I hadn't seen before. And the experience wasn't even terrible.

My face was dripping with whatever it was. I snuggled up to my pillow and closed my eyes. Some other wretch left my lips, and I was unable to stop it.

I was buggered. I pushed my eyelids close and inhale intensely.

This was buggered.

Twelve

I couldn't place the source of my awakening. There was complete silence and no glare in my peripheral vision. It was a typical day-

Despite this, there was blaring Christmas music.

My forehead wrinkled, and I drew the blanket tighter over my head, pushing it against my ears. What was happening, I couldn't even begin to guess. As much as I tried, I just couldn't bring myself to figure it out.

I sighed and cocked my head to one side. Around my legs, the blankets rustled and tangled.

After that, I hugged my knees against my chest. To be honest, I was hoping to get some shut-eye. However, the tunes kept playing. After a moan, I closed my eyes tightly.

Just not the right thing to do. It would have been better for whoever wanted to prank me to have remained in bed.

Not me; I just wasn't feeling it.

I tried to ignore the music, but I just couldn't. No matter how tightly I clamped the cloth over my ear, the noise persisted. There was an angry yell that came out of my mouth.

This can't be real. Simply put, I needed to sleep.

I took a few long breaths, searching for the calm I lacked. There was a deep impression of my face on my pillow. I started counting, got to 10, then 20.

My fingers tightly gripped the blanket I was using as a pillow.

Waiting for another five seconds, I opened my eyes. It was a whiteout. My upper back stiffened. That's when I realized that it looked like the snow outdoors that had kept me inside. In a deliberate motion, I raised my arm, pulling the white blanket covering me higher.

My eyes watered as I tried to adjust to the glare of the room's lighting. The time of day has to be early in the day.

After a long sigh, I turned over onto my back and pushed the blanket away from my face. A rustling of sheets was audible. This nightmare continued for another night. Good.

My mouth licked over its parched lips. With a groan, I lifted myself up on my left arm and swung my left hand across. My water bottle always sat on the nightstand. Without it, I would be unable to get any rest.

Whenever I did wake up, it was in the middle of the night, and I felt parched as if I hadn't had anything to drink in days. Until now, however, I hadn't. It could be related to the number of alcoholic beverages I consumed... Grasping the cold plastic, my fingers curled, and I relaxed. I propped myself up halfway, with my back against the bed rest, and opened the lid, letting it fall to the blanket below.

A frown formed on my face as I listened to the music and sipped at my drink. No, the noise wasn't originating from where I was sleeping. After a while, my eyes shifted to my door and the slight echo I could hear coming from behind it. Is there someone waiting for me outside?

I took a deep breath, downed it, and replaced the bottle on my nightstand. My feet touched the earth as

I drew the blanket to one side. It was only after taking a few steps that I realized I was still wearing my shoes.

I felt a sickening revulsion as I peered at the floor and frantically inspected my sheets for dust mites. It was time for me to pull back the sheets. Thank goodness there was no break; I'd spent the past few days inside. Nothing was visible on the pure white cloth.

I let out a sigh of relief. Thank goodness I didn't have to make a trip to the laundry room...

As it was, I could not afford to give any more to the university.

I got to my feet. I could feel my eyelids puffing out.

I crept to the entrance with tingling toes. There's no one else except Cade who could have done this, right? No one else was here saves him and myself. That's what I was hoping for, anyhow.

As I passed by the mirror on the inside of my closet, I nearly flinched. My eyelids were swollen and ringed with crimson. I let out a deep sigh. And now there was nothing I could do about it...

Instead, I focused on the entrance. My hand instinctively curled around the doorknob. I flung open the door in hopes of seeing someone there, but the hall was deserted. In the pane of glass before me, I caught a glimpse of my reflection. As I took stock of my surroundings, I frowned thoughtfully.

Nobody was around.

I took a few deep breaths. However, it did not explain why the music kept playing. I leaned forward, hands resting on my hips. It was completely dark to my left and right.

A snap echoed around the room like a speaker had suddenly gone dead. The only thing I could think to do was swallow. My eyes went upward because I recognized that sound.

There it was! I finally tracked out the origin! In the background, via the intercom system, came the music. The grey speakers mounted on the ceiling and walls made me scowl.

Cade. The responsibility for this lies squarely with him.

The answer was a resounding no, so I crossed my arms and shook my head. Was I missing the humor here? How could he not have known that I preferred to avoid seeing him?

I just stood there, still, waiting. However, I was unclear about the purpose.

Logic would dictate that he not act in such a way.

Was a justification really necessary? Cade Thindal was his name.

I think his whole point was to make me even more irritated.

My eyes closed as I felt my head spin. Now I'm finally starting to feel the effects of all the booze we drank. From our time in the principal's office, I remembered very nothing.

We had been dancing and drinking our way across the room and had ended up on the floor. He had complimented my appearance and we had even kissed, but now I realized I had to stop.

My pupils dilated and I took a clumsy step back. As I walked through the entrance to my room, my shoulder smacked against the doorframe. I braced myself against the wood as my head jerked down, expecting to see a little troll that had shoved me.

The truth was, I had kissed him.

My stomach lurched and my chest tightened as I shook my head. What the heck was I thinking?

Nothing justified my behavior except for the fact that I was... inebriated. That's right, I was so tipsy that the world seemed to revolve around me. It all made sense now.

Everything was well, and it hadn't anything to worry about. It had been nothing more than a quick peck on the lips, right? I just couldn't recall it.

I muttered an expletive, turned around, and went back inside. Putting my head in my hands, I sat down on my bed. Every song played was a festive one for the holiday season. No matter what I tried, I was distracted.

I attempted to recall the events of the previous day, but they remained hazy. I don't know what I was thinking when I chose to go out drinking with him. Holy crap, I did this.

Ugh, I moaned. It was unfathomable to me.

The music suddenly stopped, and there was a snap from the intercom. I popped my head out the open door I'd left. I frowned thoughtfully.

Like, what was he up to? Everything was running well yesterday. Clearly, he was having difficulties with it now.

The music abruptly ended after another loud snap. I let out a sigh of relief. At last, I thought my head pain would abate -

“Holly?”
I made a quip. Where are my eyes playing tricks on me? No. His words reverberated through the corridors.

He swallowed a little air. In fact, the whole university heard it. Well, it's not like you could respond to me... but, at least I hope that you can hear me, Holly... his muted chuckle reverberated.

I forced down a gulp and got to my feet, heading back out the door. My hand rested on the doorframe as I paused at the front step.

In all honesty, I had no clue where this was headed.

It was silent for a while, and I began to worry that nothing would happen. However, I was incorrect.

"Let's have a chat."

I frowned thoughtfully.

Is that his goal? Talk?

Again, his voice said, "I want you to meet me in the cafeteria this evening." Her voice lacked his usual inflection. Over the course of the last few days, he had become almost unflappably certain of his own opinions, regardless of how often he had been proven incorrect.

Sure, a few people had left, but he'd never seen anything except smiles and laughter. His name was formerly Cade.

As I moaned, my palm tightened into a fist.

Ultimately, it will be Christmas Eve. Is there any chance of a second meeting?

It was only after spending the past several days with him that I detected the hint of doubt in his voice, a little tremble. I immediately knew that wasn't him when I heard it.

I sucked my lower lip in.

It was really unusual to hear him speak like that.

"Holly, I'm sorry. Please come home so I can make things right."

-

For the life of me, I couldn't figure out what I was doing. To be honest, I didn't. I took a deep breath and kept walking along the corridors. Perhaps I was mistaken about this.

With each stride, my heart beat harder against my ribs. It had been hours since they had last seen one other. I had seen the sun begin to set, and anxiety begin to grip me. This was something I had been thinking about the whole time.

The alternative is that I could remain in bed. That was something I told myself over and over again.

But did the mistake warrant a lonesome holiday season?

After that, I shook my head. I wouldn't stay in my room if I didn't have to. The short fuse I had often caused irreparable damage.

I gritted my teeth and gripped the bag of M&Ms tightly in my fingers. Angry as ever, I was. However, I didn't like being on my own. My ego needed to stop getting in the way if things were going to go well.

To solve this problem, I would need to think it through.

Considering how much free time I had, I decided to go see him. I could always leave again if I decided I didn't like being here... This is exactly how it would play out, so yes.

After some back and forth, I would determine what course of action to take. It was ultimately my choice.

As I approached a bend to the left, I gulped. Yet, here I was... The thick doors were now the only thing hiding Cade from view. I took a few deep breaths.

At this point, it was too late to turn back.

Shaky, I used my left hand to open the door and took a deep breath before stepping inside. My stride slowed down. Something like this really threw me off guard.

It was as though my mouth spontaneously opened.

As soon as he saw me, Cade's head jerked toward me. He had gotten down on his knees close to the makeshift fort he'd fashioned out of blankets and cushions. He had a cushion in his hand. For a split second, he stopped, and then he was off and running again.

He tossed his pillow to the side and got to his feet.

He kept staring at me with a look of bewilderment in his eyes. It was awkward since I was at a loss for words. So I did nothing except stare at him in disbelief. to wait.

I really didn't expect you to show up.

Thirteen

We both felt uneasy as we exchanged tense glances. Cade took a step forward and then backed up, stroking the back of his neck as if he couldn't decide what to do with himself.

I sighed and cast an observational eye around. The customary array of tables was there, as was the open door and bright illumination emanating from the kitchen.

But I couldn't take my eyes off whatever was behind him.

Is that what you did?

This was such a dumb question that it made me want to hide under a rock. I wanted to slap myself so badly.

Naturally, he'd already taken that step. No one else was in the building save him and myself. I balled up my hand and sank my nails into my flesh. Stupid. How very foolish you are.

His lips curved up into a shy grin, and he cast a glance toward the rear. Once again, his gaze fell upon me. It took me a while to gather together enough bedding, but I succeeded.

I shifted my weight laterally from foot to foot. My neck was stiff and my jaw was clenched.

"Did you take them from your bedroom?" With an eye on his blanket fort, I inquired. Two tables spaced a few feet apart were covered with a single blanket in his arrangement. Luminous fairy lights decorated the environment.

There were a lot of pillows jammed in there. As well as, the drab, hard ground was covered by a fluffy, white covering. It took a lot of effort, but eventually, I managed to swallow and sigh.

His action showed a great deal of consideration. Also, I found it very endearing.

Finally, the idiotic smile I recognized returned to his lips. His head was cocked to one side. Some of the cushions are mine, but the rest of the decorative items belong to my neighbors. He nodded and grinned at me. You know, I've broken into my fair share of restricted areas before.

When I heard it, the pupils in my eyes dilated. "Cade-"

He laughed and shook his head. Says he, "I'll put everything back where it belongs, Holly. I swear. They won't even notice."

The furrows between my brows deepened. After pausing for a while, I finally gave a satisfied nod. There were several adjustments I had to make while living with Cade. That was already common knowledge on my end.

There was no way I could contain my laughter as I rolled my eyes. "Typical."

There was a momentary pause in the conversation. When I realized what I was still clutching, I had to bite my lip. I raised my left hand in the air. I mumbled, "I brought some M&Ms," well enough for him to hear. No idea whether I was expected to bring anything.

He crossed his arms across his chest and nodded quickly. It fits the bill well.

My heart began to beat more rapidly. It was all too much for me to handle, and I was a bundle of nerves.

As he cocked his head to one side, he pointed to the makeshift fort made of blankets. Have you decided that you want to come in?

After taking a deep breath, I nodded and let my hand drop back to my side. I squeezed by him and knelt to enter the building. I was pleasantly surprised by how comfortable this space was. There was plenty of room for the two of us, and nobody had to feel cramped. Cade followed me quickly, and suddenly we were alone in the room because he threw a blanket over the entrance. I squished one cushion behind my back and sat down in the middle of them.

As Cade shifted to the side and switched on yet another set of fairy lights, I took note. As the star-shaped bulbs brightened, I couldn't help but grin. They were strewn on the ceiling above us. It seemed like we were the only ones in the room.

like though the rest of the world didn't exist.

With a sigh, my gaze drifted to the white, furry blanket underneath me. The bowl was sitting not too far away, so I leaned back and deposited the bag of M&Ms inside. To be honest, I was at a loss for action. Also, where to begin? On the other hand, maybe it wasn't necessary.

Cade had initiated contact with me. It was his request. Moreover, he would need to understand the procedure involved. I wished it were true.

Causing me to turn my attention back to Cade, the movements to my left brought him back into my peripheral vision. He lay down silently on the ground next to me. As he tucked a pink cushion under his

head, I just gazed at him. His focus was on the string of icicle lights in the form of stars.
Perhaps I had been staring at him for too long since it was only when his head swiveled to the side that I realized he was patting the ground beside him. He glanced at me.

It's like saying, "Come and lie with me, please."

For a few seconds, I stared into his deep brown eyes. I eventually rolled over to lie next to him. I slept well because of his assistance in placing a cushion under my head, and then stillness descended once again.

All of a sudden, the atmosphere surrounding us relaxed. There was still the sense that we were both at a loss for where to begin. However, at this point, we both had the same understanding. No harsh words or rage were exchanged. Simply what I've come to accept as inevitable chaos and label ambiguity.

As I took a few deep breaths, I focused on the twinkling lights. It was like peering up at the stars... As an alternative to staying in my room, this was far more enjoyable.

Even if the worst had occurred, I wouldn't change a thing.

I'm sorry, Holly," Cade sighed.

When I let out a breath, my mouth parted. I mean, "For what?"

Just hearing him say it satisfied my curiosity about the nature of his apology. Inexplicably, I felt the desire for it. Something like a proclamation, I guess.

He put his palm up to his head and shook his head. "I dunno, Holly... I assume it's for messing up? I see now that my previous comment was incorrect.

Not a peep out of me. As though he still had more to say, it seemed as if words were floating aimlessly just below us.

To top it all off, I aimed to give him some breathing room.

I didn't see this coming..." I-I was afraid that I'd be alone by me again this holiday season and-" I thought I caught a sigh on his part. I thought my heart was going to cease beating. Back on your own?

"I took you by surprise."

There was a momentary pause in the conversation. My heart was now hammering against my rib cage. It slammed into my ribs and I felt the impact. Again by

yourself?" I inquired. My eyes widened and my head cocked to the side as I studied him.
In a low voice, he said, "Fuck," and he shut his eyes. To calm himself, he brushed his fingers over his face and eyes. "Did I just say that?"

Understanding that he couldn't see it, I nodded my head in agreement.

He whispered something under his breath as he licked his lips. My brows knitted together in concentration, but I said nothing more. Time was something I attempted to offer him.

I saw that he eventually let go of his hand and let it fall back to his side. He peeped his eyes open but avoided meeting my gaze. He seemed to be marveling at the decorative lighting. "This is my second Christmas spent at the hotel."

It seemed like my windpipe was closing up on me. I was at a loss for words.

His lips curved into a grin, and he sighed contentedly. He abandoned me before I was born, so I never knew him. Also, I lost my mother four years ago.

As my heart sank, an icy chill radiated across my chest.

Three times he blinked.

I lived with my stepfather and her before I went to university. In the past, we always had parties together.

A moment of stillness passed before he finally shut his eyes.

And now that she's gone, he doesn't seem to have any interest in me at all. This is the preferable option. When I left, he seemed relieved to see me leave.

"Cade-"

To cut me off, he shook his head. "No. There is zero compassion or anything like that. I needed to get it out of my system, and perhaps you can benefit from hearing it.

There was a shift in his head position. When he looked at me, I could see that he was smiling through the tears that were forming around his eyes. I'm sorry, Holly, he said softly. It was quite naive of me to think that my issues were unique. What I said to you was hurtful, and I apologize.

He had only one tear drop down his face. I smiled at him and reached up to brush it off. The words "it's OK" came out of my mouth in a low whisper. It finally clicked for me. Even I have my down moments.

He shook his head, his hand coming out to grip mine. I wasn't sad, Holly. I just-"

"During the holidays, I find myself thinking a lot about my dad, even though I try not to."

He pursed his lips and looked at me intently. After taking a few long breaths, he sighed. It's possible that my envy had a role... In the days leading up to the snowfall, I couldn't stop wondering "what if?"

He released his grip on my hand. For Christmas, you would have gone to be with your loved ones. And there I would have been, all by myself."

My soul ached for him.

And Holly, I'm f***ing sorry you have to spend this time with me right now. This is something that I would never want on anybody.

I said softly, "I don't want to be anyplace else."

He froze and fixedly looked at me. I flattened my left hand between us as I lay on my side. That's why I waited. After a moment of confusion, he grasped the concept. There was a tangle in our fingernails. I gave him a warm grin and a tight grip on his hand.

This caused me to laugh out loud. Why do you suppose I wanted to go at such an ungodly hour? Anyway, I didn't feel like seeing my stepfather.

His attempt at a grin was something he was struggling with. Our eyes met, and we stood there, transfixed. His eyes and freckles were like a galaxy I'd seen. I felt like I couldn't help but grin ear to ear.

To put it simply, I was relieved that things had worked out this way. Christmas would have been ruined for both of us if we had kept arguing. We still had each other, despite all that had gone wrong.

Epilogue

"Cade!" I yelled.

He regarded me with a cocked eyebrow. "What?"

I shook my head and moaned, "I swear to god." If the blankets catch fire, the speaker says, "If this..."

The response was emphatic: "No, Holly, it won't."

The hair on the back of my neck sprang on end as my eyes narrowed and my head jerked up to look at him. He had gotten the chocolates from the kitchen and carried them inside the fort. There was a definite gloom in the air since the sun had set an hour or so earlier.

But the fairy lights saved the day!

He flicked the switch on the green lighter in his palm and lowered it. Several candles that he had brought with him lit the space between us. As soon as I set eyes on them, my pupils dilated.

The possibility that he was attempting to set the building on fire remained. The truth is, I could see it happening. Occasionally, he might be so erratic.

"It'll all work out," he said with a grin. He looked at me for a second before returning his attention to the candles. He lighted the first one, and I saw the spark in his eyes instantly.

There's snow all around us even if this does spark a fire. If we were to simply leap into it, we'd be rescued.

“Cade!” I yelled, extending my arm to smack his. He was shocked, but then he laughed. A split second later, he arched an eyebrow in my direction.

He reached down and picked up the lighter. You're truly putting out the fire of the one who started it? And here I was supposing you were timid!

Laughing, I shook my head. Put an end to that hogwash and shut talking about it. If we leaped into the snow, we'd perish!

When he bent down once again, he did it with a sneaky expression on his face. After he finished lighting the candles, he set the lighter down and reached for the marshmallows.

Did I explain how the marshmallows made it into the cooking area?

I raised an eyebrow and shook my head.

His lips began to crinkle into a smile. I told you that this is my second time staying here, but I assume you didn't realize that nobody ever leaves food in the kitchen during breaks.

His head cocked to the side. He reached inside the bag and pulled out a marshmallow, which he promptly speared with a fork. I took it from him and he immediately began working on his own.

"I found it out last year," he beamed. The fact that I wasn't stranded here meant I could go grab some groceries. And I became wise to my errors."

The sight of the marshmallow being held over the flames of the candles caused me to gape at him.

The cheese, crackers, marshmallows, cacao powder, and other pantry staples were all stashed away by me. It's not like you touched it, did you? He was beaming a smile at me.

I felt my cheeks warm up ever-so-slightly, and a tinier grin formed on my lips. At this point, I have no idea why I should be ashamed of myself.

It might have been him, after all.

I said, "I don't like cheese," as I brought my fork closer to the flames. I was feeling tentative and even bashful.

With a snort from Cade's nose, he moved his left hand to scratch behind his ear. As he stared at me, his eyes lit up like little fires. "I figured,"

A moment went by. Waiting impatiently, I stared into the candle flames as my marshmallow became golden brown at the rims. To prevent it from burning, I shifted it to the side.

Cade laughed out loud and shook his head. We may thank me to the moon and back, Holly because that was a fortunate break. What if I hadn't done that? Without the outside help, we surely would have perished here.

A shiver ran through me and I bit my lip.

The guy was correct.

What may have occurred if not for Cade was too terrifying to contemplate. I said with a grin, "Thank you, I think," but I still found this whole thing quite off-putting. To be honest, I was tormented with what-ifs. I felt chills go up and down my body. Had that happened, I would have had to rely on whatever I could scrounge up in my room.

And to think, this morning was my first exposure to the M&M packaging... Nothing good could have come of it.

We quickly devoured the marshmallows and other sweets he had provided. After what seemed like minutes or hours, we were back on the fluffy blanket.

Once again, we found ourselves transfixed by the enchanting illumination.

There was pleasant stillness for a while.

In addition, I offer you this:

When I felt Cade's gaze on me, I cocked my head to the side. Smiling, he moved away from me and then back to me. I burst out laughing as he gave me a little, greyish item.

"My phone?" After reading this, I had to laugh.

It was a low, muffled "Yeah" on his part. You left it in the office of the school's principal. Leaving it there would have been a horrible idea.

My throat felt tight and I couldn't swallow. I burst out laughing again.

Oh my God, just think if she had discovered it after we had finished all her booze.

Cade shared the humor. Once again, I turned to look at him.

I said, "I'm sorry." In other words, "I can't give you anything..."

Smiling and shaking his head, he acknowledged me. Saying, "Holly, you've arrived. All I need is that."

I ascended and shifted to the side.

I bent over him, peering into his eyes with a broad grin on my face. Like the stars in the cosmos, they shone brightly and were a golden color. A little frightened, he did nothing while I laughed at his expense.

My internal monologue went something like, "You're such a fool," as I lowered myself. When I saw his eyelids shut, I kissed his face and then his forehead. I bent down and smiled while gazing at his thick, black lashes. When he finally parted his lips, I inhaled his warm, familiar air.

My focus immediately went to his mouth. The question, "May I kiss you?"

When his eyes landed on mine, they widened suddenly. For an instant, he looked at nothing but his eyes. Then he cracked a grin. The moment has finally come, and I can't wait. He gripped my head with his fingers and lowered me.

As our lips touched, I felt the air leave my lungs. None of my wildest Christmas Eve fantasies had come true. Even so, I hoped for the best.

www.ingramcontent.com/pod-product-compliance
Lightning Source LLC
LaVergne TN
LVHW010610160826
845677LV00013B/3342

* 9 7 9 8 3 6 6 8 7 5 2 2 6 *